THE ALBION CHRONICLES
Prequel

Queen of Betrayal

Also by Nelly Harper:

The Albion Chronicles:
The Girl of Two Worlds
Seven Druids
The Battle of Brigantia

******

The Jet Necklace

The Albion Chronicles

Prequel

Queen of Betrayal

By

Nelly Harper

The Albion Chronicles
Prequel
Queen of Betrayal
Published by Goblin House
www.goblinhouse.co.uk
Paperback
ISBN: 978-1-9996229-0-9

www.nellyharper.co.uk

Queen of Betrayal

He could make out almost every blade of grass in the clearing. Not even the green woodpecker with her camouflaged feathering was hidden from him. What he wanted to see, however, was deep within the surrounding woodland, beneath a thick, leafy canopy. The trees did not hinder him for long. A breeze was all it took to move the leaves aside so that his eagle eye could catch sight of the various movements below. Warriors were lurking in the heavily wooded, steep banks of the ravine - waiting.

The woodpecker stopped probing the ground for ants and lifted its head. Something had disturbed the peace. With flashes of its yellow rump, it flew, low and undulating, until it disappeared from sight. Moments later, the first wave of legionnaires appeared. They had not seen the warriors lying silently in wait, although they were expecting them. In the past, the Romans had found such tactics impossible to predict and defend but this time the battle was planned.

The two sides came together in a clash of swords and shields. Birds and the few small creatures still remaining fled in terror as the deafening cries of the carnyces filled the air. The legionnaires stood their ground, not letting the noise and the unpredictable nature of the fighting unsettle them. They had their orders; this time, the rebels would not succeed.

Bodach could see that all was not well; Caradoc was doomed to lose. Even Belatucadros, Albion's god of war, had begun to sense it. Enveloped as they were now in the red mists of battle rage, the warriors could not hear his warnings.

The gods had been complacent in the years running up to the invasion, believing this island to be a safe haven. They had not felt the danger until it was almost too late. The Romans were a formidable force and backed by gods just as greedy for the acquisition of lands as the Roman leaders themselves.

Some of those foreign gods were here now, inspiring the legionnaires to fight harder. Mars and Minerva had both made their presence felt. Bodach could feel it; a cloying heaviness in the air. He ruffled his feathers, hoping to free himself of the taint.

Beneath him, the fighting was fierce. Caradoc, once joint leader of the Catuvellauni and now war leader to the Ordovicii, was relying on the nation's wild and hilly land to protect them yet again. It was one of their best assets. For a number of years, they had used the natural cover of the ground to spring surprise raids on unsuspecting cohorts. The regimented legionnaires had no way of defending against such hit-and-run attacks. Now, though, the Roman governor, Publius

Ostorius Scapula, had forced them into open conflict and Caradoc and his warriors were at a disadvantage.

The discipline of the Roman army soon ensured they had the upper hand. Warriors fell in their hundreds; even Caradoc's wife and daughter were not safe. They were dragged from their hiding place and taken prisoner. The legionnaires were not gentle with them, nor were they honourable. Just like every woman the legionnaires captured, the two were treated as chattel and subjected to the urges of the bawdy fighters.

Bodach was the Wise Old Man; he had watched over Albion for as long as anyone could remember. It tore at his heart to see those defending it being cut down in such a way. He could have flown away, left his eagle guise and returned to the ether, but he forced himself to stay and watch as the Ordovicii, and the Silures who had joined them in the battle, perished. His consort, Cailleach, was the wisest of them all. She had tried to warn the gods long ago that the fates were weaving mischief into their webs. She flew to him now, in her guise as a raven. Jet-black feathers to his eagle browns. They tumbled downwards, falling closer and closer to the tree tops. His eyes searching below to see what it was that she trying to show him.

The ground, stained red with the blood of the valiant warriors; who had tried, but failed, to defend their territories against the might of

Rome, was far from silent. Legionnaires, busy searching the dead and injured for spoils, laughed and joked. Here and there, men cried in pain whilst others cried in shame and frustration. Shouts and orders rang out as those prisoners still able to walk were rounded up into small groups, ready to be herded back to camp.

One warrior had broken loose from the others. Keeping to the darkest shadows, he crept silently away, leaving the carnage and slaughter behind him. Only Bodach's vision was keen enough to see the determination on his face. This was no cowardly retreat. It was the last defiant act of the warleader. Caradoc was fleeing for help.

***

'I see no problem with the name Britannia.' Cartimandua waved away her husband's concern. 'It is only a name, what does it matter?'

'What does it matter?' Venutius almost choked on the words. 'It is our land and its name is Albion. It has always been so. What right do these… invaders have to change it? Would you have them change the name of our nation? Shall Brigantia now be called… Little Rome?'

Cartimandua rolled her eyes and sighed. 'You bore me, husband. You were quick to accept the hand of friendship when the Romans first arrived. Why all this drama now? Are you not happy that our land is at peace?'

'I would not have our people at war.' Venutius rubbed a hand over his face. 'But the cost? Taxes are one thing, all these changes are another. We are no longer the keepers of our own truths. What will they interfere with next? The Silures and the Ordovicii may well have the right of it. What good is peace if we are no longer our own people?'

Cartimandua threw back her head and laughed. 'I can assure you, I am my own person. I choose the paths I take, the paths my nation takes. I say the Romans can only bring us good fortune. Those who oppose them are fools, too blind to see that progress is necessary. This new name merely confirms that the old ways are dead, just as those who continue to cling to them will be.'

Venutius shook his head; he despaired of his wife and her love of the Romans. She was blinkered by their promises and the riches that she believed would be hers if she continued to facilitate them. He looked to the corner of the room, where Galchobhar stood, unspeaking. His brown druid's robes swept the floor as he turned to face the wall. He pressed his forehead against the cool timbers.

Keep your tongue, my friend. The goddess's voice sounded in Galchobhar's mind. *There are trying times ahead. You will do no good by angering her now.*

The voices behind him faded into the distance as he focused on her words. It saddened him greatly that Brigantia, the goddess who had given her name to the nation, should be so wary of her own queen. Galchobhar had hoped that when Cartimandua married Venutius of the Carvetii, her obstinate nature would be tempered. It had not happened. Cartimandua, born to royalty and spoilt as only royal children can be, had no intention of softening to anyone. It was her duty to marry so marry she did but she saw no reason to listen to her husband any more than she listened to anyone else.

Galchobhar turned back from the wall in time to see Cartimandua stride from the room. Venutius was still shaking his head. 'What did you do to me when you tied me with her?'

'Your marriage brought stronger friendships between the Carvetii and the Brigantes, and raised you to king of the largest nation in Albion, my friend. To which end the people are very happy. I am only sorry you are not.'

Venutius smiled at the druid but it was a smile that failed to reach further than the corners of his mouth. 'Would you be happy with such a woman?'

Galchobhar opened his hands, 'I believe I chose my calling wisely.'

This time, Venutius's smile reached his eyes. 'I believe you did. You and my brother both have the right idea. Though the only thing stopping Epillus marrying is his own stubborn nature.'

Venutius's brother had travelled with him from their old home at Dunmallard, along with a small group of men. They were Venutius's staunch friends and allies and all were as worried as he was. Even amongst the Brigantes, talk was often of the warriors standing up to the Romans in the south.

A contingent of Brigantes had held their own uprising a few years earlier but it had soon been quashed. Ostorius had sent legionnaires to aid the Brigantian army and the rebels had been quickly defeated. Peace had returned but clearly the feelings of disquiet were not buried as deep as Venutius had believed. The more he heard, the more he now found himself agreeing with them. He looked to Galchobhar; he knew the druid was as concerned as he was. 'You look worried, are the gods still unsettled?'

'The firmer the Romans' foothold on Albion, the stronger their gods become. Each time they are invoked, the more their essence chokes the air. Soon, the people will be encouraged to accept these new deities and turn away from the ones we have always held in our hearts. I worry that Cartimandua will even lose her faith in the High One, Brigantia.'

'Surely that will never happen. Cartimandua is stubborn and in awe of what the Romans can give us but she would never turn her back on her own goddess. For a queen to do such a thing would be tantamount to treason.'

They were interrupted by the sound of shouting filtering into the room. Cartimandua's voice issued forth, demanding that her guards seize someone. Footsteps rushed past and another voice - male this time, with a lilting southern accent - pleaded with her to listen to him. Venutius and Galchobhar rushed outside. A large crowd had gathered, drawn by the commotion. In its centre, a shabby, travel-worn man had been forced to his knees. Two guards stood holding on to him, making sure that he could not rise. In front of him, Cartimandua stood, her face hard and unrelenting.

'Caratacus, you are no friend of mine,' Cartimandua told him, purposely using the Romanised version of his name. 'You shall find no shelter here. I will not put the safety of my people at risk to harbour nothing but a rebel.'

***

'You know what they will do to him? They will parade him through the streets of Rome; make a spectacle of him and his family. They do not deserve such treatment simply for trying to protect their own lands.'

'They should have surrendered to Ostorius,' Cartimandua spat. 'It is no concern of mine, Venutius, if Caratacus was too blind to recognise the might of Rome, to foresee the greatness that we are all now a part of. He has sentenced his wife and daughter to death.'

'And worse! Does that not bother you?'

8

Cartimandua snorted her derision. 'They are a lesser family, nothing to wrinkle your brow over. They would have held on to the Catuvellauni had they only accepted Rome's hand of friendship as we did. That Caratacus's wife and child chose not to denounce him as a traitor is their own misstep. They have brought their fate upon themselves. Why should I have sympathy for such fools?'

'What is this "Caratacus" nonsense? His name is Caradoc. Why must you insist on using these Roman names?' Venutius's voice rose, 'You are blinded by your obsession with the Romans. Take heed before it is too late. The people will not suffer such a behaviour.'

Her voice rose to match his, 'The people will accept the will of their queen. Our actions have kept them safe, brought wealth to our nation and good fortune to all.'

'Galchobhar would not agree with you.'

'Galchobhar is just being petty. He cannot possibly expect me to bar priests from crossing onto our lands. They do him no harm. He seeks to challenge me at every turn these days.'

Venutius halted his pacing and stared at his wife. It was one thing to criticise Caradoc and his wife, but to criticise a druid - her archdruid at that - was unthinkable. She looked at him, one eyebrow raised mockingly. 'You think I should heed the druid's words instead of those of Ostorius?'

'Only a fool would ignore a druid's warnings.'

'Ostorius came to our aid three years ago, when those peasants rose up to cause us trouble. He has been a good friend to us. Have you forgotten that so quickly, husband?'

'Such a good friend that he then stationed some of his troops permanently on our lands?'

Cartimandua threw up her arms. They had clashed over this particular point on numerous occasions. No matter what arguments Venutius put forward, she could see no harm in having the legionnaires so close.

'He even gave you your arms-bearer, and what better man have you had?'

Vellocatus was indeed an exemplary arms-bearer. Venutius could say nothing against him. Cartimandua did not even pause to see if he would answer. 'You have accepted the governor's hospitality, his friendship and his gifts, yet you expect us to turn our backs on him now and hide this fugitive? A fugitive who, I might add, has caused the people of Albion much consternation.'

Obviously they each got their news from different places.

Cartimandua pressed on. 'The people do not want the old ways. They want the advancements that Rome can bring: the baths, the sanitation and the roads.'

'The people want to trust their leaders, to know that when they come to them for aid they will not be turned away.'

'Caratacus,' Cartimandua emphasised every syllable, 'is not one of our people. He is nothing more than a rebel.'

Venutius's patience was at breaking point. 'Caradoc is fighting for Albion, you cannot hand him over. He came to you for help. What kind of a queen are you?'

Cartimandua's eyes were blazing. 'I am faithful to my allies. Caratacus has brought war on them and now he seeks to drag us into that war. I will not have it. He will find only chains here.'

'And my voice is to be unheard!' Venutius almost roared the words at her. She smirked at him, unmoved. His patience snapped. He slammed his hands down on the table as he rose from his seat. He would not strike her but he could no longer trust himself to remain in her vicinity.

It was clear when he left the room that their heated exchange had been overheard by many at the fort. Guards and servants stared at him wide-eyed in disbelief. He pushed past them and hurried to the hall. In the height of summer, the two large fires had not been lit and it was dim inside. Galchobhar joined him a few moments later, striding into the room with such purpose that for a moment Venutius thought he was coming to challenge him. The druid's hands clenched into fists, opened, and clenched again. He was so beside himself with anger that he could barely form his words.

'High One be saved,' he finally got out. 'Can she really be serious? She would turn over one of our own? Why can she not see sense?'

Venutius dragged a hand across his face. 'She is blinded by wealth and power. I can no longer reason with her. What good is the backing of the Carvetii, when she has the Roman Empire?'

Galchobhar calmed himself with some effort. He laid a hand on Venutius's shoulder; he could feel the despair coming from the man, whom it appeared was now king in name only. 'There is no reasoning with her when she gets like this.'

'Her demands are getting worse. She sees nothing but that which would advance her in the eyes of Ostorius.'

Galchobhar nodded his agreement. He turned from Venutius and spat into the hearth. 'There is a sour taste in my mouth and it cannot be taken away by a piece of their sweet fruits.'

Footsteps outside made them pause; a guard ducked his head into the hall. He saw the archdruid and the king, nodded his head and moved on. Only when his footsteps had faded into the distance did Galchobhar resume talking.

'The poison that is filling our land is getting stronger, my friend. We must convince her to change her mind.' He remembered Brigantia's earlier warning. 'Arguing is not the way. We must placate her, even if it burns our tongues to do so.'

'It will certainly burn mine,' Venutius frowned. The pressure he had felt building for many moons had now settled on him as a great weight. He could see no way forward if Cartimandua went ahead with her plans.

***

It took almost a turning of the moon for the Romans to arrive at Almondbury. During which time, nothing Venutius or Galchobhar said made any difference. Their only hope now was that Cartimandua was stringing them along for her own amusement. It would not be the first time she had done such a thing.

The name Cartimandua meant "sleek pony" and she had been well named. Never before did a queen sit a horse so well. She sat now, astride her favourite pony in the entrance of the palisade, watching as the Romans drew nearer. Her stomach lurched as one of the riders pulled in front of the others. So it was true; he had come. She lifted her chin a fraction higher, her back already ramrod-straight. Beside her, Venutius tried to keep the glower from his face.

At her other side was Galchobhar, his brown hair hanging loose to his shoulders. His beard, though shaggy, was well kempt. He fingered it now as he watched the governor smile in greeting.

Inside the hall, Ostorius reached out a hand and clasped Cartimandua's. Raising it to his lips, he kissed her knuckles. His eyes, when they met hers, lingered a heartbeat longer than propriety dictated.

'Publius Ostorius Scapula, we are most honoured by your presence. I had not thought that you would bother yourself with such a tiresome journey.'

Ostorius waved a hand, 'It is worth all the trouble when the prize at the end is such a fine one.' It was not clear which prize the Roman governor was referring to.

Around the hall, those gathered to witness the handing over of the prisoner stiffened. Up in the rafters, a barn owl watched with her clear, unblinking stare; too high for anyone to see the unusual green of her eyes. Galchobhar had felt her presence the moment he had entered. If Verbia was here then this must truly be the start of something new. She was the maiden goddess; daughter of Brigantia the great mother, granddaughter of Cailleach the Crone. Where they represented motherhood and protection, age and wisdom, Verbia was the impetuousness of youth. She was at the start of all things; joy, innocence and hope. Would this be the day that Cartimandua finally stood up to the Romans?

Beside Cartimandua, Venutius stood forward to acknowledge the governor. He was stony-faced, his deference to Ostorius only just masking his animosity. Cartimandua paid him no attention. She was sick of his complaining. When the Romans had first invaded Albion and announced their intention to stay, she and Venutius had agreed, together, to accept their terms of alliance. To put the wellbeing of their large nation above all else and not to fight. It had proved over and over to be the right decision. They enjoyed a good relationship with the governor and had the backing of the Roman army in times of trouble. Why her husband should waver now was neither understandable nor acceptable.

'How was your journey? Did the weather hold?' she asked.

'It was long and, I confess, tiring but the weather brightened with every passing day. I swear even the sun god, Sol, regards you in good stead.' Ostorius inclined his head towards Cartimandua. Venutius risked a glance towards Galchobhar, who rolled his eyes.

Oblivious to the exchange, Cartimandua threw her head back and gave a false, tinkling, laugh. 'Would you like to see the prisoner?' She clapped her hands and immediately the large doors at the back of the hall opened and four guards came in, bringing Caradoc. He was still in chains, though someone had taken the time to ensure that he had bathed and dressed in clean clothes.

Ostorius looked mockingly down his long, aquiline nose. 'Caratacus, how fortunate.'

'My name is Caradoc.'

Ostorius's face hardened. 'I do not hold with localised names. From now on, you will be known as Caratacus. You will be taken from here to Camulodunum, where you will be reunited with your wife and daughter. You will then be boarded onto a ship and taken to Rome.'

Caradoc did not respond, though his face

showed relief at the knowledge that his wife and child still lived. He had expected that transport to Rome would be his punishment. He was the leader of an insubordinate nation and he had caused Emperor Claudius much consternation. Naturally, Claudius would want such a high-profile prisoner to be paraded through the streets of Rome; to be jeered at and humiliated, so re-enforcing the message of what happened to those who chose to stand against the Empire.

Galchobhar glanced again at the rafters. The owl was still there. *Where is the learning in this?* he silently asked her. *What good could possibly come from such a heinous action?*

Wait and see, Galchobhar, for not all things are obvious at their conception.

Cartimandua lavished attention on Ostorius during the remainder of his visit, making sure that he wanted for nothing. Each evening, she laid on the best foods, having entertainers brought in from far and wide. If she noticed that not everyone was happy with her actions, she chose not to acknowledge it. Venutius held his tongue; there was still time.

All the while, Caradoc was kept under close guard. Venutius had Vellocatus watch and report if there was any possibility that they could somehow release him. He reported back that at least three legionnaires stood watch night and day. There would be no chance that anyone was going to be able to free Caradoc before Ostorius carted him south. The next day, the guard was increased to four. Venutius noted a smirk on his wife's face when he entered the hall. He kept his mouth closed and for the first time began to doubt the loyalty of his arms-bearer.

Ostorius stayed at Almondbury for half a moon's turn. When he was finally ready to leave, they gathered at the huge wooden gateway in the palisade wall surrounding the fort. Caradoc was dragged forward and pushed onto a cart, to which his bindings were firmly fastened. He was afforded a little movement and a thick sheepskin to sit on. Claudius wanted the pleasure of parading a noble through the streets of Rome; it would do them no good to mistreat him before he got there. Venutius stepped up to the cart. 'I am sorry that it has come to this, Caradoc. It was not of my doing.'

Caradoc gave a weak smile, 'That is probably the last time anyone will call me by that name. Other than my wife and daughter, that is.'

Ostorius gave a call and the group began to move. The cart creaked as the wheels turned, bumping the warleader of the Ordovicii from side to side. A legionary jumped up beside him, his sword held flat across his knees. The message to the prisoner was clear but Caradoc had no intention of trying to escape. Cartimandua had been his last hope; the only reason he had fled after the battle had been lost and his wife and daughter captured. During his incarceration, some of the legionnaires had

taunted him with tales of rape and mistreatment -
so much for hoping that their status would
protect his loved ones. The risk he had taken had
not paid off; there would be no support against
the Romans now. Caradoc would not desert his
family again; they would face whatever the future
held together.

The gates were being dragged shut behind them
when Galchobhar pushed his way to stand in
front of the queen. He was shaking with rage.
'This is a dark day for all Brigantes,' he told her.
'Our goddess looks down on us with tears in her
eyes. You have shamed the High One, our blessed
Brigantia.' He pointed his finger towards
Cartimandua's face. 'Your love for the Romans
will be your undoing. You will drag this nation
into war with your actions.'

Cartimandua glared at him. 'I have saved this
nation from war. It is time you asked your
goddess why she wants to bring death and
destruction to her people. The Romans want
nothing but peace.'

Galchobhar staggered backwards, his worst
fears realised. In the stunned hush that followed, a
voice from the crowd cried out, 'They want our
taxes.' A number of others rose up in agreement.

Cartimandua held her hand up for silence. 'You
would put a price on peace?' she called out. 'If you
would fight the Romans, make sure you leave my
lands first. You are no longer welcome here.' She
glared at Venutius. 'That goes for you too,
husband.'

As she whirled around to leave, Galchobhar found his voice again. 'I curse you, Cartimandua, Queen of the Brigantes. I curse you and your Roman alliance. I curse you in the name of Brigantia, Cailleach, Verbia and Bodach. Of Maponus, Cernunous, Belatucadros and Nodens. All the gods of Albion stand at my back as I curse you.' He bent and scraped together a handful of earth and threw it in her direction.

Cartimandua continued to walk away, head held high as his malediction fell on deaf ears. She entered the hall with her guards. The door shut behind them with a resounding thud.

Venutius looked at Galchobhar. 'Enough is enough,' he told the druid. 'I want my marriage ended. I cannot stay joined with that woman. She is no longer any wife of mine.'

Galchobhar nodded. 'I will speak with the gods.'

Vellocatus stepped away from him. In three strides, he had reached the hall door. He did not look back at Venutius before opening it and disappearing inside.

***

Back in her private rooms, Cartimandua laughed as she poured out the contents of the chest Ostorius had quietly given her. Gold and jewels glinted in the firelight. She pinned an ornate golden fibula onto her tunic and patted her hand over it. Her husband was a fool if he thought she would turn away such riches.

There was a knock on her door. Annoyed, she threw a rug over the jewels, hiding the chest, and called for the person to enter. Her guards would never let anyone get so close if they meant her harm. She was surprised when Vellocatus entered. He bowed his head in respect.

'Ostorius requests that you accept my services as yet another gift of thanks for your loyalty.' He nodded his head to the table, where the glint of gold could just be seen peeking out from beneath the rug. 'He hopes that you enjoy the chest.'

Cartimandua hurriedly tugged the covering into place. 'Your services are my husband's to enjoy.'

'Venutius is leaving. He has asked the druid to annul your marriage.'

Did Venutius think she was a trinket to cast aside when he saw fit? How dare he! Her hands clenched into fists. Cartimandua eyed Vellocatus thoughtfully. 'Tell me; just how was it that the governor knew my husband had been insisting I did not hand over the traitor Caratacus?'

Vellocatus smiled, 'The governor is not a stupid man. He knows that agreements made before the full extent of Rome's ambitions are known do not always hold. He has eyes everywhere.' His own glinted. 'I am his eyes here, and we both like what we see.'

Cartimandua's interest was piqued; maybe Venutius leaving was not such a bad thing. She stood and walked towards Vellocatus. 'I should have you flogged for such a suggestion.'

Vellocatus stood his ground; he had been looking at the queen inappropriately for weeks now and she had never once reprimanded him. Even now, she thought she had her smile hidden, but he could see it. It was in the straightness of her shoulders, and the tilt of her head; the careless raise of her eyebrows and the slight curl at the corners of her mouth. She trailed a hand across his chest.

'I should have you killed for admitting to being a spy.'

Her face was little more than a handspan away from his now. He made himself look contrite. 'Not a spy against those loyal to Rome, my queen. Merely a messenger to warn against possible infraction, so that the governor can take steps to... smooth out the problem, before it becomes... a problem.' He looked her straight in the eye. 'Would you like to punish me... some other way?'

For a moment, Cartimandua was too shocked to answer; there was no mistaking what he was insinuating. She pulled her hand back, as if burnt. Flirting was one thing but this was unacceptable. She had never been approached so blatantly before, and certainly not by someone barely higher than a servant. She slapped his face, hard. 'Where is my husband now?'

Vellocatus's cockiness vanished; he had pushed his luck too far. He bowed again; lower this time. 'I presume he is in his own rooms, packing his belongings.'

Cartimandua's face lit up as if a hundred candles were reflecting on it. Vellocatus had always thought her beautiful; now he was in awe. She swung away from him and called for some wine. 'The best we have,' she told the servant. 'I am celebrating.'

She waited until her glass had been poured and handed to her, before looking at Vellocatus. 'Should you not be preparing to leave?'

'I have no intention of leaving my queen. Ostorius would have me stay here with you and keep you safe.' Again he bowed. 'If you would have me, that is.'

'Would he, indeed? Is he worried that I might decide to follow in my husband's footsteps and begin to question his authority?'

Vellocatus shook his head. 'He is not worried about your loyalty in the slightest, my queen. It is your safety that concerns him.'

Cartimandua's insides flipped over. The governor excited her like no other man ever had.

'Publius Ostorius Scapula likes to look after those who serve him well. Venutius has vented previously that he would not remain at your side, should you hand over the traitor Caratacus. Ostorius would not have you left unprotected.'

Anyone would think that Cartimandua did not

possess guards of her own. Still, she was not going to dwell on that point. It was enough that Ostorius was concerned for her welfare. Cartimandua sipped her wine and tried not to lose herself in the possibilities ahead.

She had not thought of it before but as marriage had made Venutius king, once it ended, so would his claim on the title. She would be the sole ruler of Brigantia. She stroked the fibula again. As far as she was concerned, her husband and his followers could not leave soon enough.

'In that case, I welcome you, Vellocatus.' She smiled and poured him a glass of wine. 'But you must be mindful of your position. Do not seek to overstep your station again.'

***

When Venutius rode out of Almondbury, Galchobhar was at his side. As were his brother, uncle, and a number of loyal servants. He had discouraged many others from joining him. They needed to safeguard their homes and livelihoods; besides, he would need loyal eyes and ears in the fort to keep him informed of Cartimandua's behaviour. He no longer trusted her to act in the best interests of her people.

It was early evening when they saw the ragged slopes of Dunmallard in front of them. Venutius sighed. When he had left here years before, he had never envisioned returning under such circumstances. In the distance, he could see the unmistakable glint of water. Squeezing his eyes together, he tried to make out the banks where his fishing boat had been kept.

He had always loved this place; his whole childhood had been spent here, hunting in these woods, fishing in the Wolf Water. He had spent hours watching the fish hawks hovering above the lake before swooping down and crashing right into the surface, feet first. Many a time, he had seen them beating their wings furiously as they dragged a huge trout clear of the water. In his eyes, there was no more beautiful place in the whole of Albion.

'It will be good to be home,' Torrigan, Venutius's uncle said, riding up alongside him. 'I have not seen my wife and children for a number of weeks.'

Venutius inhaled the scent of the nearby gorse. Cailleach was obviously still watching over him or he would not be able to smell it. 'It will indeed.' His uncle was a good man; he divided his time between Dunmallard and Almondbury; not the easiest of ways to raise a family.

A yellowhammer cried out its distinctive call, warbling away at the end as if it had run out of breath. 'Ah, I have missed this place.' Venutius threw a look over his shoulder. 'Shall we race?' Urging his horse on, he broke into a canter. Not waiting to see if the others had joined him, he pushed her even faster, until they were galloping flat-out along the track to Dunmallard. At the bottom of the hill they slowed, his mare blowing her breath out and tossing her head. He patted her on the neck; she was such a loveable horse – sure-footed and always eager to please.

By the time he had reached the large gates of Dunmallard fort, the others had joined him. 'I call that an unfair race,' Torrigan berated. 'You caught us off-guard.' He laughed and clapped Venutius on the shoulder. 'I should have known that you would try such a trick.'

'You were always a bad loser, Uncle,' Epillus called as he reigned in his own horse. 'My brother, as I remember, started from a standstill, whereas your mare was still walking.'

Torrigan grinned, shrugging. 'An old man has to have his pride. You two would strip me of it every time we do anything.'

Venutius looked to his brother, feigning shock. He tried to keep his face straight as he nodded to his uncle. 'We will race at a trot next time, to preserve your decrepit bones.' He wheeled his horse away quickly before Torrigan could reach and give him the clout such a comment deserved.

'That is a fine humour to arrive home in,' a woman called out to them. 'And it is a fine humour everyone will be in when they see you have arrived so unexpectedly.' She reached out and took hold of Venutius's reins.

'Mother.' He jumped down and dipped his

head to her, before she gathered him into her arms. 'I had not thought to see you until Samhain at least,' she said when she finally released him. She rushed over to Epillus and hugged her younger son. Venutius might be a king but Epillus was just as special in her eyes.

Epillus was quick to notice the new limp in her step. 'You are hurt, Mother. You should not be on your feet.'

Waving away his concerns, she linked her arms through both her sons' and proceeded to lead them into the hall. 'It is nothing to worry yourselves over. Dolnoach has been treating me.'

'And what do you think of the new druid? Uncle tells me that he is very young.'

Annagh released hold of her sons as she ducked into the hall. 'He is still finding his feet; replacing Candetas has not been easy for him. Dolnoach is a very different druid, and it takes time for the folk to adjust. But I think they are coming around to him, slowly.'

Candetas had been the druid at Dunmallard longer than most people could remember. Cailleach had finally called him to the afterlife in the spring of that year, just after the equinox. His replacement was a druid of Belatucadros. This had caused some alarm amongst the residents of the fort; Belatucadros was the god of war and strife. No one at Dunmallard wanted unrest. It made them wary.

Inside the small hall, servants hurried to set out food and wine for the newcomers. The plates and goblets were plain compared to those of Almondbury but Venutius barely noticed; such things were only important to Cartimandua. He sat on a carved oak chair, listening to Epillus and his mother chatting.

'You are quiet,' his mother said after a while. 'I see worry behind your eyes.'

'I have set aside Cartimandua, Mother, and come home. Would you have us stay for a while?'

Annagh's face grew strained. 'So, the talk has been true? She has handed over Caradoc? I must admit, I have half been expecting you to appear ever since I first heard the rumours.'

Venutius rubbed his face with his hands. 'The woman is impossible. I tried over and then some, to reason with her. But she will hear nothing against her blessed Romans.'

Annagh leaned forward and took his hand. She rubbed it between her own. 'You have tried, my son. I admit, just like yourself, I thought that these Romans would make good allies. But they have not settled. They do not want to live in peace; they want to consume us all. I am only glad that we Carvetii are too small to attract their attention yet.'

'Cartimandua and I have never seen eye-to-eye on much. She is only happy when she is getting her own way. In truth, we have lived almost separate lives since the uprising a few years ago. It has taken all my tact and diplomacy to keep a civil tongue in my head with her, but this... this was too much. Caradoc came to us for help, Mother. We were his last hope. The Romans have decimated his lands, the Ordovicii all but wiped out. Only the Silures stand against the Romans in the west now. I fear Ostorius will stop at nothing until he has conquered the whole of Albion.'

'Galchobhar cursed her,' Torrigan told Annagh, entering the hall. He poured two goblets of wine. 'Out in front of everyone. I have never seen him so angry.'

Annagh's eyes widened and one of her hands flew to her mouth. To be cursed by a druid was no small thing. 'What did she do?'

Torrigan shook his head, 'She ignored him. She just turned and walked away, leaving him shouting at her back.'

Silence followed his words. No one ever ignored a druid. Annagh looked to her sons, as if one of them would deny Torrigan's words. When no one did, she finally let out her breath. 'What did Galchobhar do? I see he is not with you. Is he still at Almondbury?'

Annagh had only met the Brigantian archdruid once, on the day he had performed the wedding rites between Venutius and Cartimandua. She remembered him as a tall, stern man; not someone that anyone would ever wish to cross.

'I must leave these two to explain,' Torrigan said, taking the goblets. 'I wish to see Penyah before I forget what she looks like. Hopefully if I take her wine she will not be too cross at me for being away so long this time.'

'You will find your wife weaving, if I am not mistaken. She has missed you.' Annagh nodded to him as he left, quickly turning back to her boys. 'Well?'

'Galchobhar left Almondbury with us, he will be here shortly. He has ridden on to the nemetons. He needs peace for a day or two, to commune with the gods and find out what they would have us do.'

Annagh was relieved. She did not relish the prospect of facing him while he was still mad with anger at Cartimandua's slight.

'Fear not, Mother,' Epillus said, 'He is not as ominous as you seem to think. He is a good man; Brigantia would not have him for her druid if he were not. Now, tell us more about this Dolnoach. Surely he is the more frightening?'

Annagh tried to smile. 'He is a little reserved and very formal but he is personable in his own way. He is also at the nemetons just now. The dark moon has called all the druids home…' Her words trailed off. She was not the only one in the room to be thinking the same thing. Could it be that the gods had been expecting this trouble?

✳✳✳

As promised, Ostorius sent labourers to improve facilities at Almondbury. They arrived a

29

few weeks later, bringing with them a magnificent bay stallion. He was the colour of the water that flowed from the peat bogs at the far end of the moor, with a mane and tail as dark as night. A gift, she was told, for accepting Vellocatus as her new protector.

Cartimandua was in raptures; she had always loved to ride. She took the stallion out that very day, urging him faster and faster over the moors. The wind tore her hair from its bindings and made her breathless but the ride was too exhilarating to stop. Only when the stallion was lathered in sweat and breathing hard did Cartimandua finally pull on the reins and bring him to a slow walk.

She ran her hand down his neck. 'I shall call you Scapa,' she told him. 'After Ostorius Scapula.' Inside, her heart quickened and her pulse raced. It was nothing to do with the gallop.

She dropped from the horse and ran her hand up his nose and forehead. He blew out his breath and pushed his head against her. She laughed, 'We are going to be good friends, boy, are we not?'

Scapa nudged her again and then dropped his head to pull at the grass. Cartimandua looked around. The moor was bleak and, to her mind, beautiful. She could hear the chatter of wheatear, filling the air with their sharp little calls. Farther away, a number of curlews probed the ground with their long, curved beaks and a hen harrier hovered in the sky, its owl-like face focused intently on the ground below.

Cartimandua had spent her childhood riding out over these moors. Never had she felt more free than when she was out alone, exploring them. Now she longed to bring Ostorius here, to point out her favourite views and feel like they were the only people in the world who mattered. They had ridden together often during his previous visits, though there had always been a retinue with them. The governor, it seemed, travelled nowhere without his guards and hangers-on.

Scapa pulled methodically at the grass. Cartimandua patted him on the neck. 'Come on, boy, time to go home.' She gathered up his reigns, grabbed a handful of his mane and threw her leg up and over his back.

Back at Almondbury, she dragged a comb through her hair, staring at her reflection in a small, bronze mirror. What was it Ostorius saw when he looked at her? She was not as young as she once was but she was still beautiful. Vellocatus had told her so only that morning.

Cartimandua smiled at the memory. Maybe the Roman did not understand that, in Albion, servants did not offer such compliments to their masters? She shook her hair out again and let her mind drift.

She saw herself riding across the moor, Ostorius at her side. Not a wild ride this time. This one was slow and they had plenty of time to admire the beauty all around them. She imagined Ostorius helping her down from Scapa, tenderly taking her in his arms and kissing her. His hands, soft and warm, covered every inch of her body until she longed to cry out. She gripped the table tightly, her breathing shallow and fast.

There was a brief knock at the door and Vellocatus entered. Cartimandua's cheeks were flushed, her pupils dilated and her pulse much faster than normal.

'Did you enjoy your ride, my queen?'

'I did. The horse is magnificent.'

He stepped a little closer. 'You should not go riding alone. You must let me come with you next time.'

Vellocatus was young and handsome, still in the prime of his life. Cartimandua could not help herself; she imagined him in place of Ostorius. She blushed, turning away quickly.

'Is there something about your ride that I do not know, my queen? That is a pretty colour to turn for no reason.'

For once, Cartimandua was at a loss for words. Vellocatus was standing very close. She could feel the heat from his body and her breathing quickened. Never before had she felt such feelings. Her intimacy with Venutius had been perfunctory at best; the few other encounters she had experienced had been not much better. Vellocatus took another step closer. She turned to face him. Why not? she thought. She was queen, after all. She could do whatever she wanted. Convention could go and rot.

The west of Albion was in uproar. The treatment of Caradoc and his family had not gone un-retaliated The legionnaires were subject to a constant barrage of attacks, harassment and intimidation. Ostorius answered the disquiet with promises of annihilation. The Ordovicii had already been decimated so it was their neighbours, the Silures, who now bore the brunt. The governor sent a large force of legionnaires into the region to build a number of small forts and stamp their presence on the land. The Silures attacked with such ferocity that the Roman force was almost decimated. Ostorius was beside himself with rage. Britannia was his island; he would not be defeated by the barbarian tribes who still clung to the old name.

He sent more and more legionnaires to the west, determined to quell the rebels. He should have taken the time to learn about the people he was up against. The more Ostorius promised their total destruction, the more united the area became. Smaller nations neighbouring the Silures entered into the fray, along with a number of men from farther afield.

Venutius, Epillus and Torrigan were quick to join them. They spent a year fighting alongside the warriors, becoming ghosts in the hills and valleys and giving Ostorius no peace whatsoever. Time and again, the rebels attacked the legionnaires. Often they grabbed hostages, spiriting them away and scattering them amongst the smaller tribes, far out of Ostorius's reach. If the governor had thought that the capture of Caratacus would quieten the rebellion, he had been very much mistaken. The stress took its toll.

In Brigantia, Cartimandua revelled in her solitary status. Her relationship with Ostorius, which had started to look so promising, had faltered, his attention taken by the west. Cartimandua sent gifts and words of support and received similar in return but the exchanges were always brief. She kept Vellocatus close, though she did not repeat her earlier dalliance. He was her link to the governor and as such he was as precious to her as Scapa.

She was out riding the horse one late spring morning when she saw a number of riders working their way along the valley beneath her. She squinted against the bright sun and saw snatches of crimson and gold. Romans. Giving Vellocatus and her other guards no warning, she raced back down the track the way they had come. She could not meet Ostorius whilst smelling of horse and looking so windblown.

Her maids had just finished fixing the braid in her hair when she heard horses clatter through the gateway. Giving her cheeks a pinch to add some colour to her pale face, she hurried to the door. Her heart clamoured in her chest. Ostorius had sent no warning of his imminent arrival and, whilst she was not averse to surprises, she would have delighted in the excitement of anticipation had she been told that he was coming.

Vellocatus appeared at her side. He too had taken the chance to smarten his appearance. He gave her a wink but she hardly noticed it. The horses were pulling up in front of her. Ostorius was not amongst them. Her heart plummeted. One of the legionnaires jumped from his horse and dropped to one knee.

'My Queen. I bring grave tidings. Publius Ostorius Scapula is dead.'

***

Cartimandua was beside herself but whether it was grief or annoyance, it was hard for even her to tell. She had fallen for the handsome governor the moment she had first laid eyes on him. His dark, curly hair and olive skin - so different to her husband's - had excited her senses.

Her relationship with Venutius had not been a love match; their marriage had been strictly strategic - an alliance between Brigantia and the Carvetii. She had quickly grown bored. Venutius was serious and loyal but he could not see past the duties of his predecessors.

Cartimandua had no time for preserving the sanctity of the past. She wanted to rush headlong into the future with open arms; to revel in the advancements that the Romans brought with them. She wanted the sumptuous bath houses, the heated buildings and the grandeur of the architecture that the Romans were producing. With every message she had received from Ostorius, her anticipation had grown. She had longed for him to return to Almondbury but the troubles with the Silures had escalated to such heights that he had been forced to concentrate all his efforts on defeating them. It had not stopped Cartimandua from hoping.

The news of Ostorius's death shattered all that. Gone was the man she loved. Gone, the opportunities his favour could bring. The new standing she would have acquired as his wife would never happen, and the steady trickle of gifts that she had become so used to would be no more. She had gaped at the messenger, unable to form any words. Vellocatus had stepped in, taking over and offering the men the hospitality and friendship the queen would normally provide. For once, Cartimandua had not complained. She had let herself be led away to her quarters, where she had slammed the door on her maid and torn the room apart.

She did not emerge for three days. When she finally stepped out of the door, the messengers were gone and life, for everyone else, was just as it had ever been. Cartimandua called for Scapa. She rode slowly through the settlement that nestled beside the fort, inside the safety of the heavy palisade walls. The women were hard at work, weaving on looms in the doorways as their small children played in the dirt close by, enjoying the autumn sunshine. Men were up on the roofs, repairing the thatch and making sure that they were ready for the harsh winter to come. The air was filled with happy voices. Cartimandua could even hear singing coming from one or two of the houses.

Her mood grew dark. When Venutius had left, all these people had been downcast for weeks. Ignoring Vellocatus's warning, Cartimandua set Scapa towards the gateway in the palisade and tightened her legs. The horse needed no other signal; he tossed his head in the air and trotted forward, scattering children right and left. Once she was out on the open moor, Cartimandua leant forward and let the horse fly. The wind rushing into her face pulled tears from her eyes and whipped at her hair but she did not care. Eventually, when the trees crowded in around her, she slowed and let Scapa get his breath back.

She looked around her and realised that she did not know where she was. In her mad flight, she had paid no heed to where the horse was taking her. Did the gods hate her so much? Was she to be lost in everything? A sound in the undergrowth startled her. A brock, grown fat on that year's bumper crop of acorns, was rooting around for grubs. It was unusual to see one out in daylight and she stared, fascinated. The brock paid no attention to her and went on snuffling through the leaf litter.

Cartimandua saw the bushes all heavily laden with fruit and noticed that the leaves on the trees had only just begun to fall; all the signs pointing to a hard winter ahead. The men were right to be getting ready; the brock, too. She looked back at him. He lifted his head finally, his beady black eyes peering straight at her. She was caught in the moment then the brock turned away and the interlude was broken. Were the gods speaking to her? She watched the brock as he carried on foraging. It was as if he had not even seen her, as if her presence meant nothing.

Ostorius's presence had meant nothing to the people of Almondbury. Only she, it appeared, had been affected by his death.

The sound of hooves filtered through her thoughts. Turning, she saw Vellocatus riding towards her. 'My lady, you have been gone for hours. I thought something had happened to you. It is not right for you to be out here alone.'

But I am alone, she thought; *apart from the brock.* She glanced over her shoulder just in time to see it disappearing into the bushes.

Vellocatus reined his horse in next to her. 'You will not bring him back by harming yourself.'

Cartimandua opened her mouth to snap a retort but closed it again when she noticed the concern on his face.

'You are not the only one to feel such pain, my lady. Britannia has lost a great governor; he will be missed by many. The Silures and their supporters have a lot to answer for.'

Cartimandua had been so focused on her own loss that she had not stopped to consider the wider repercussions of Ostorius's death. Her mind flicked to Venutius; she had heard that he had joined the rebellion. Old resentments stirred - had the man who had once been her husband killed the man who should have been? She took a deep breath. 'How did he die?'

'It is said that he died from the strain of dealing with the rebels.'

Cartimandua could not help the slight feeling of disgust that welled up inside her. She had presumed that Ostorius had died an honourable death, his sword in his hand, fighting the rebels. Never for one moment had she entertained the possibility that he could have been taken by anything so mundane and... pathetic. She had thought Ostorius was stronger than that. He had certainly covered his weakness well.

They rode back to the fort in silence, each lost in their own thoughts. For Cartimandua, the bubble had burst. She could see now that she had just had a lucky escape. She had already suffered one marriage that had let her down; she did not want to tie herself to another man who fell short of her requirements, whatever his title.

Beside her, Vellocatus was wondering how long the queen would let him remain at her side. He had seen the revulsion in her eyes. She had wanted the governor and anything connected with him when she thought Ostorius was a strong man. Now that she knew otherwise, would she cast him aside?

The palisade had just come into view when a dog ran out from nowhere to bark at the horses. Scapa took fright and lunged forward. Cartimandua grappled with the reins, pulling the horse into a tight circle to stop him running on. Undaunted, the dog bit out at Scapa's front legs. The horse reared up, throwing Cartimandua from his back, and took off down the track, the dog hard on his heels. The air was knocked from Cartimandua's lungs and pain radiated from her ribs. She lay where she was for a moment, her eyes closed tight against the pain.

She groaned and her eyes flickered open. Vellocatus was already at her side, urging her to move slowly. 'You win,' she told him when she could finally speak again. 'I should not come out here alone.'

With a lot of help, Cartimandua got to her feet. She was only on them a moment when her knees buckled and she would have fallen had Vellocatus not grabbed hold of her. 'You are in no fit state to walk or ride, my queen. You must sit upon my mare with me.'

Somehow, he managed to lift her onto his horse and hold her steady whilst he climbed up behind her. The horse walked at a sedate pace, mindful of her precarious load. Cartimandua tried to sit with her usual grace but the pain was almost unbearable and she soon found herself slumped against Vellocatus. She could smell sweat and horse mingled together. It was not unpleasant. Neither was the feeling of the strong body at her back and muscular arms around her, holding her close.

They found Scapa farther down the track; he had a cut to his hind leg and was limping badly. Vellocatus caught up his reins and the horse hobbled along beside them.

Cartimandua closed her eyes. It had been a long few days and she really needed some comfort. She thought back to that illicit night they had spent together, just after Venutius had left. She wished that she could repeat it now; maybe it would fill the void that had opened up inside her at the loss of Ostorius and the future she had planned with him?

'You must not worry, my lady,' Vellocatus murmured behind her. 'You are quite safe; I will never let you fall.'

***

'Sire, I have news.'

Venutius looked up to see Dolnoach standing in the doorway; he waved him inside and offered him a stool by the fire. 'You would do well to wear a warmer cloak.'

The druid looked down at himself in surprise. Apart from the thick flakes of snow covering his shoulders, he could see no problem with the garment. He pulled the stool away from the hearth, removed the cloak and laid it across his knees to dry out.

'Do you never feel the cold?' Venutius asked.

Dolnoach flicked his straw-like hair from his eyes and studied the two men before him. As usual, Epillus was with his brother. The two had just returned from hunting and had been discussing the failing reliability of one of their hawks.

'Firstly, the cold is not something to be abhorred so. It is a necessary part of the cycle of the year; it should be embraced as such. Secondly, if the bird is so loath to hunt for you, why do you feel the need to keep it tethered in your aerie? Gift it back to the gods whence it came. There are plenty more birds to be had.'

Epillus felt a shiver run down his spine. They had not been speaking so very loud; the druid could not possibly have heard their conversation unless he had been spying at the door. Yet he knew that could not be the case. Their uncle had only just departed; he would never have left an eavesdropper standing there.

Venutius also shivered but it was the thought of embracing the cold that bothered him. He had never been fond of the winter months. The thick flakes of snow and biting wind were only marginally better than the icy rain that would no doubt follow. He sipped at the rapidly cooling mulled wine in his cup.

As if he could read his thoughts, Dolnoach looked at Epillus. 'Your uncle is not nearly as discrete as you are. I presumed that when he marched past me just now muttering about a useless bird, he was talking about one of the hawks. It would, after all, be the prudent thing to assume, given that you have all just returned from hunting.'

He cast his eyes to Venutius, dismissing Epillus with a bemused shrug. Venutius pulled his chair closer to the fire.

'What is this news, Dolnoach?'

'The new governor, Didius, has been seen travelling south again. He stayed at Wendell for three weeks this time. Word is that he was there to attend a wedding.'

Venutius looked up sharply. 'Whose wedding?'

'Cartimandua has married your old arms-bearer; the one given to you by Ostorius. It seems she has had her fill of Almondbury for the time being. Wendell is to be their home now.'

'Has she lost all reason? The people will never stand for such a thing.'

Dolnoach shrugged, 'Apparently that is why they requested that the governor be at the ceremony. The blessing of Rome cannot be denied - or so I am told.'

'It would appear Vellocatus has more to him that he let on,' Epillus said, pushing an iron poker into the fire. 'I always said I did not like the way that he looked at her.'

'You did that,' Venutius agreed. 'I am inclined to believe more than ever that you and Galchobhar were right about him.'

'I am always right,' Galchobhar interrupted, ducking into the room. He poured a cup of wine and held it out towards Epillus.

Epillus sighed and pulled the glowing poker from the fire, thrusting it into the wine. It sizzled as it heated the ruby liquid, then again as he thrust it back into the fire. Galchobhar poked at the film of ash that appeared on the top of his wine before downing the drink in two large gulps. 'Now, what was it I was right about this time?'

'My once wife has married again.'

'It has been over a year, my friend. It is not so surprising.'

'Beneath herself this time,' Venutius told him. 'She has married Vellocatus.'

Galchobhar stared at him. 'Has she gone mad?'

'We had no children so she is free to do whatever she wants. I do not care who she takes to her bed but the people will hardly suffer him to be their king.'

The three of them turned questioningly to Dolnoach, who nodded slowly, 'The reports are that she has indeed named him her king.'

'Bitch!' Venutius slammed his cup down with such force that it shattered in his hand.

Epillus finished re-heating his own wine and placed the poker back on the hearth. 'You will always be thought of as king, brother.'

Venutius smiled at him, 'You misunderstand me.

I do not care about the loss of my title. Cartimandua could have chosen to name Vellocatus as her escort only but in naming him king she has effectively raised a low-ranking Roman over the heads of every high-ranking Brigantian. It would never have been accepted had he not had the backing of the governor. Aulus Didius Gallus clearly has no scruples. They are showing the people that even the lowliest Roman is worth far more than they are. In short, they are stamping Rome's authority over Brigantia in no uncertain terms. Now, should anyone rise up against the Romans again, they will be doing so against their own king.'

'Treason.' Galchobhar shook his head and sighed. Treason was a far more serious crime than rising up against neighbouring rulers. It was punishable by death. 'I fear that my curse has taken the slow route to fruition.'

'The circle turns, my friend, fear not.' Dolnoach turned the other side of his cloak towards the fire to dry. 'Every step Cartimandua takes is another step towards her downfall. I feel Belatucadros growing more and more restless.'

✷✷✷

Aulus Didius Gallus was a far different governor to Ostorius. For a start, he chose to concentrate on developing the lands that the

Romans held in Albion, rather than expanding them. The Silures, however, refused to be ignored. Whilst the rest of Britannia gained new roads and buildings, the west of the region remained as turbulent as ever, forcing Didius to continue building forts as bases from which to repel the rebels.

Annagh worried for her boys; she could see how restless Venutius was becoming. No matter how much she advised him against it, he visited Brigantia frequently and each time he returned, his anger had increased further. She longed for him to find peace at Dunmallard but his years as the Brigantian king could not be put aside. He despaired for the people and he despaired for the gods. The more he heard of how Cartimandua and her new husband were acting, the more he boiled with the need for action. Epillus, still committed to his elder brother's cause, followed him everywhere. Annagh feared her sons would never settle down and give her the grandchildren she longed for. They would not be happy until the Romans were driven from Albion but she could not see that ever happening.

The brothers still travelled down occasionally to help the Silures, coming back with terrifying tales of their clashes. One time, they brought five legionnaires back with them, to be held as hostages. Torrigan and Epillus took the men deep into the Carvetii lands. On the biggest of a group of islands in the middle of a large lake, they left the captives in the hands of the druids. Steep-sided fells covered in oak woodland surrounded the lake, cutting it off from the rest of the nation. Even if the legionnaires could somehow escape the druids and swim across the water, they would have no idea which way they had travelled to get there.

It was said that Belatucadros himself was often seen, sporting a pair of fine antlers and dancing wildly in the frequent torrents of rain that blessed the area and kept its many lakes filled.

Torrigan and Epillus were in fine spirits as they made their way back to Dunmallard. They were just within sight of the hill when riders caught up with them, bearing a Brigantian banner.

***

'What do you mean they have been taken hostage?' Venutius roared at the young messenger. He picked his glass up and hurled it at the wall. 'By the grace of the gods, what reason does she give for such an action?'

'M... m... my lord,' the boy stammered. 'She s... says to keep the p... peace, sh... she will hold them. Sh... should you s... stop your ins... surrection and leave the Romans to their b... business, then they will c... come to no h... harm.'

Venutius hurled another glass.

'It will do no good to kill the messenger,' Galchobhar said, taking the boy to one side and giving him a stool. 'Now, tell me. Did the queen say anything else?'

The boy nodded his head, his nervous eyes twitching back and forth between the two men. 'Sh... sh... she says you... you... you brought this on y... your... self. H... heed the p... promises you made to R... Rome, r... return to your a... a... ag... greeable s... state and your family will l... live in l... luxury. F... f... fight a... and th... th... ey will d... d... die.'

The boy took a huge gulp of air to recover from the struggle of getting his words out. His face was flushed from the effort it had taken. Galchobhar ruffled his hair. Cartimandua, who had no time for weakness of any kind, must have chosen him especially to deliver the message, thinking that she was being amusing. He hoped that she had not done anything to the boy's parents to get him to comply.

Venutius raged up and down but resisted the urge to throw anything else. Annagh came in and took the boy away to be fed. He ate everything she put before him but refused to accept any further hospitality. After another long struggle, he managed to make her understand that men were waiting for him at the bottom of the hill, to escort him back to Wendell.

'I cannot stand for such an affront, Galchobhar,' Venutius stormed when the boy was gone. 'I do not trust her word.'

'What can you do?'

Venutius sank onto a chair and rubbed his face. 'By the gods, I do not know what to do. I would have my family back. Torrigan's wife has just presented him with a fourth bairn. I am told it was a difficult birth; she has not recovered fully. She needs her husband, just as the children need their father. As for Epillus…' His voice trailed off.

'We must think about this carefully,' Galchobhar advised. 'I will speak with Brigantia.' He rose from his stool. 'Though Dolnoach may have the better answer - Belatucadros has been growing more and more unsettled of late.'

'As well he might.' Venutius looked severe. 'I would be happy to place my trust in him right now.'

The water lapped on the pebbles, distracting his mind from its turmoil. Galchobhar focused on the sound, regulating his breathing into slow, steady breaths. He had wanted to walk to the stone circle but time was of the essence. Instead, he had tucked himself away on the banks of Wolf Water, beneath an overhanging alder tree that stood with its roots in the lake. It was out of the sight of Dunmallard and not a place where they were likely to be disturbed. Brigantia would not mind being called to such a beautiful place. Out on the water, a grebe caused a tiny splash as it ducked down under the rippling surface. At the same time, unseen, a barn owl flew like a ghost to alight on the tree.

'Brigantia is not the one you want.'

Galchobhar looked up. Verbia stood, her feet in the water. He bowed his head briefly before speaking. 'There is trouble brewing in Brigantia, I sought the goddess to ask for her guidance.'

'The trouble is known.'

It was not often that Verbia was unsmiling but today her face was blank. She was testing him. Galchobhar's heart thumped in his chest. There was meaning in her appearance; how did it relate? He felt his way forward cautiously. 'Venutius would free his brother and uncle but to do so would cause unrest in the nation.'

'Unrest is already in the nation.'

'Venutius would not cause the people harm; he only wants his family back.'

'That is not true.'

This time, the maiden goddess's voice was sharp. Galchobhar flinched. He had not prepared himself fully for this meeting; his mind and body were not as settled as he would have had them. Ordinarily, he would have preferred a day or so of solitude and reflection, to rid himself of the noise in his head, but time was a luxury they could no longer afford. With Cartimandua now married to a Roman, the people of Brigantia were feeling more and more oppressed. Her actions against Caradoc and now Venutius were abhorrent. The people needed someone to fight for them, someone to rally behind.

Galchobhar's heart leapt - they needed a leader.

Verbia smiled. 'There is no one better, my friend.'

The druid's thoughts raced on, indifferent to the fact that Verbia could hear every word. Venutius would rejoice in the knowledge that the gods supported his wish to rescue his family. Cartimandua had torn a wound in him when she had turned her back on Caradoc and clasped hands with Ostorius. It shamed him that he could ever have been married to her. Now she had taken away his brother and uncle, it was more than any man should be forced to bear.

Galchobhar felt his pain. He too had supported Cartimandua in the beginning; had thought her a fitting queen for their great nation, even with her stubborn nature. As archdruid, he had failed in his duty to advise her. Despite all his words and warnings, greed and selfishness had got the better of her. It had twisted her soul and buckled her reasoning. Now the fortitude she was famed for was serving Rome's favour and not their own. Still, he was certain that, for all the animosity, Venutius had not thought to stir up an army.

'Venutius is someone they trust. Give him the mantle of Albion to wear about his shoulders, Galchobhar. Ride at his side and let my mother's people see that we have not abandoned them.' Verbia reached up and snapped a branch from the tree, cleaning the twigs away until she had a neat wand in her hand. She passed it to the druid. 'Take this wand of Fearn; let it give you strength for the challenges ahead. Remember, Galchobhar, whenever you feel weakened, like the wand, you only need immerse yourself in water to be strengthened. But unlike the alderwood, yours should be the water of the soul.'

He took the wand, feeling the power pulse through it. Alder trees were known for their protective qualities when the future was uncertain. It was for this very reason that he had chosen this place to call for Brigantia. Verbia caressed his cheek. 'You have a long way to go, my friend. We have faith in you. This is a new time, a new path for you both. It will be rocky but this land is worth fighting for.'

Galchobhar smiled. The maiden's touch had invigorated him. He felt instilled with a vigour and certainty he had not felt for a long time. The gods had got it right yet again. Verbia was just the one he needed to instil the drive and confidence required to move forward. 'We have bowed down long enough and allowed Cartimandua's maltreatment to continue. We will do it no longer.'

'Never forget, you have our blessings.' Verbia lifted her arms. In the time it took Galchobhar to blink, she had disappeared, and the barn owl was once more perched on Fearn's branch. The owl's pointed gaze bored into him for a moment then her wings opened and she was flying.

Less than a moon later, Venutius had raised a small army and was marching on Wendell. Cartimandua was unconcerned. She had known that Venutius would react with aggression. She knew how close he was to his family; his brother, especially. She had already sent word to Didius for help and he had provided a number of auxiliary cohorts to guard the prisoners.

The initial confrontation was sharp but Cartimandua held her ground. It pleased her to see Venutius's face fall when she informed him that his family were not in fact being held at Wendell. Instead, they were at Winco, in the very south of the region. What did not please her, however, was the following that Venutius had gathered. She had always known that he was a popular man but to raise an army against her - even such a small one! She felt a grip of fear tighten inside her. The second Venutius left, she sent an urgent appeal to Didius for more help. The governor, annoyed at the inconvenience, sent Caesius Nasica with the IX Hispana legion. It was a four-day hard march before they arrived, during which time Venutius had moved his army south.

They found the fort of Winco heavily guarded by Roman auxiliaries. Even worse was the discovery that, tucked into the surrounding woodland, the Maiden's Well, which had been worshipped as far back as anyone could remember, had been desecrated. The holly and rowan that had protected the site had been cut right back and an ornate stone statue of a Roman goddess now stood above the bubbling water. This only served to fuel the anger that the Brigantians were feeling against their queen. They lost no time in smashing the idol, flinging each small piece as far away into the woodland as possible.

Winco sat atop a steep hill, further protected on all but the steepest northern slope by a ditch and outer banking. The banking, being much less than the height of most men, was easily scaled. The auxiliaries guarding the fort had pulled back behind a second, much higher, rampart encircling the top of the hill, safe in the knowledge that the warriors could not pass this far more formidable defence.

Their confidence was soon tested. The wood-laced stone that made up the rampart was easily fired. The heat was intense. Thick smoke filled the air as the flames licked their way through the fortification. Stone cracked and the walls caved in on themselves as the stone vitrified. Inside the ramparts, the auxiliaries were left with no means of escape. They braced themselves for the battle to come.

Venutius and his warriors launched their attack whilst the fires were still burning. The auxiliaries, outsmarted and outnumbered, gave up protecting their hostages and fought for their lives. The cell that the prisoners had been housed in backed almost onto the ramparts. The roof had been in flames by the time rescue had reached them. As the door was forced open, one of the supporting beams collapsed, landing on Torrigan and engulfing him in flames. Epillus flung himself across his uncle, smothering the fire. Epillus and Venutius hauled Torrigan from the ruin and carried him down the hill to their camp, where Galchobhar could treat his injuries.

The burns were mostly superficial, though the side of his face was badly blistered and his hair was almost all gone. Galchobhar cooled his skin with stream water and applied soothing plantain poultices. Then he turned his attention to Torrigan's leg. It had taken the brunt of the impact from the beam and was hanging at a sickening angle. He gave Torrigan a handful of willow bark to chew on and waited for the pain relief to take effect.

The scream as the druid pulled the leg back into position could be heard all the way back up Winco hill. The fighting there was still going strong. The auxiliaries had been taken by surprise at the ferocity of the attack and had only just held their own. Darkness finally forced the two sides apart. Down in the attackers' camp, Dolnoach met with Venutius and his brother.

'We cannot call it a victory. We have your brother, uncle and the other hostages, but the Romans have held the fort.'

'What is left of it.' Epillus looked up at the smouldering remains of the ramparts.

'I do not like destroying a fort - a border fort least of all - but it had to be done.' Venutius clapped his brother on the back. 'You would have done the same for me, no doubt.'

Epillus laughed. 'Aye, I would, though I would not have been able to raise an army to do it.'

Dolnoach disagreed. 'One mention of Venutius's name and the people would have rallied. Look at them today. They have longed for a chance to take up arms against the Romans. Had we canvassed further, the number of warriors would have tripled, at least. Cartimandua may hide behind her excuse that the alliance with Rome keeps her people safe. Reality has shown that it has pushed them into war.'

Epillus's mouth was agape. 'Are we at war, brother? Did our lives mean so much?'

'The gods tell us that it is not only your lives which needed rescue. Brigantia would have her nation back and it seems she has chosen me to lead the people to freedom.'

They were woken the next morning by a carnyx blaring a warning. The IX Hispana had arrived, cutting off any chance of an early retreat. Caesius Nasica proved a far better commander than the one leading the auxiliaries. Still, the fighting did not all go their way. The legionnaires were career soldiers, their lives dedicated to serving and fighting wherever they were ordered to do so. The

Brigantians, along with the handful of Carvetii who had joined them, were fighting for their honour. They had suffered years of subjugation, humiliation and lack of voice. Now they were making themselves heard and no one could mistake what they were demanding.

The fighting carried on for a number of days with neither side able to claim outright victory. Eventually, exhaustion and lack of supplies forced Venutius to withdraw his men. Their challenge may have come to an unfavourable end but their determination to drive the Romans from Albion had not diminished.

***

'They have sent him back to Rome?'

Vellocatus stamped his feet and rubbed at his thighs. He had been riding for days, he was stiff and cold and not in the best of humours. 'It is said that he asked to leave. He was unhappy with Britannia and so has been withdrawn. The new governor, Quintus Veranius Nepos, made it clear to us that he did not seek the position. Rather, he was given it on the merits of his previous achievements. He has already called for action against the Silures. He will not repeat Didius's mistake of simply trying to maintain the peace. He intends to stamp his authority on

Britannia and increase her borders.'

Cartimandua looked concerned, 'Will he cause us trouble? There has been no word of anything further from Venutius but I do not expect that we have heard the last of him.'

'We have accepted a strong legionary presence in Brigantia ever since Venutius's uprising. They are here to help us as much as to keep peace for the governor. Veranius will not seek to disrupt us. He intends to start his focus on the Silures.'

Cartimandua relaxed a little. She was still not fully over the illness that had prevented her from travelling south with Vellocatus when the summons came. She'd had the uneasy feeling that she had lost favour with the old governor, now that the people of Brigantia had become unstable. Hopefully, this new man would be more like Ostorius and see her for her true worth. She had married a Roman, uniting their two sides even further. What more could she do to prove her loyalty to Rome?

If Veranius was determined to prove that he was not the weak governor he considered his predecessor to be, he started well. Not only did he benefit from a distinguished military career, he had also been appointed Augur, by Emperor Claudius. Augurs were an elite branch of the Roman priesthood, whose predominant role was to study omens. They specialised in discerning information from the flight patterns of birds, interpreting dreams, and reading the entrails of sacrificial animals. From the very start, Veranius determined that there were presences in Britannia which needed to be eliminated.

In order to stamp his authority on the province and clear it of its recalcitrant ways, he embarked on a number of objectives: the obliteration of the Silures; the uniting of the Roman and Albion gods; and the mitigation of the power held by the druids.

His predecessors had had little joy with the druids, finding them belligerent and unmovable, encouraging the people to think for themselves and hold faith with their ancient gods. They held sway over the seasonal celebrations, presided over disagreements and tribunals, and held the final word on all the important issues of the day. Veranius simply drove them out.

As soon as the Roman-held territories were free from the druids' influence, Veranius launched a campaign to show the people of Britannia just how similar the Roman gods were to their own. No longer were they forced to decide between one or the other; Veranius matched the closest of the gods together and simply "forgot" about the rest.

In the west, the Silures were subject to a number of well organised and co-ordinated attacks. Finally, after all their years of dissidence, their stubborn resistance began to crack. Unluckily for him, Veranius cracked first. His heart gave out after less than a year and Britannia found itself once again needing a new governor.

As bad as Veranius had been, his successor was far worse. Gaius Suetonius Paulinus was a name that came to represent dread on the lips of everyone opposed to the Romans' occupation in Albion. Barely had his feet touched land when he made his presence felt. Britannia shuddered under his wrath. That he abhorred the druids' very existence was obvious from the outset. Those not already in hiding were soon fleeing in terror.

The Albion gods despaired as they saw the druids relegated to the island of Ynys Môn. The air in the southern part of Albion was now thick with the taint of the Roman deities. Veranius might have convinced the people that the gods were one and the same but his words had been false and held no truth. The Roman gods dominated, made all the stronger by the priests that had flooded into Britannia.

Suetonius was not content to let the druids live in sanctuary on their sacred island. As Veranius had divined, the druids were the dark presence that had previously proved so hard to defeat. As far as Suetonius was concerned, they were the reason that this land had seemed cursed and so full of ghosts and spirits. With the druids gone, the legionnaires need no longer fear the misty valleys and magic-filled forests. He marched his men west and attacked with all the fury of a man possessed.

Galchobhar and Dolnoach felt the devastation

of the gods long before the first refugees arrived in the area. They retired to their respective retreats to await word of what had happened. Brigantia recovered first and after many hours of waiting, Galchobhar finally learnt the truth. On the sacred island, the druids were all dead. The groves had been destroyed and the shrines smashed. Only a handful had got away, using coracles to cross from the tip of Ynys Môn over the sea to the Carvetii coast. The gods had watched the massacre and although Belatucadros, Camulus, Andraste and a number of other victory and war gods had given their all to help, they had been unable to hold back the legionnaires for any length of time.

Suetonius had brought priests with him, who had invoked their own gods: Mars, Minerva, Nerio and Virtus. All powerful gods, who between them had already helped the Roman armies to dominate so many new provinces.

Brigantia could barely speak. 'Find the survivors, find them and help them. For without you all, we will be lost.'

Belatucadros had been even more precautionary. It was almost midnight on the second day before he finally came to Dolnoach. By that time, Galchobhar had already left for the coast on his rescue mission.

'Hold back,' the war god told his druid. 'Now is not the time to move against these demons. There is already an uprising in the south, Boudicca of the Iceni has gathered her forces and is moving against the Romans as we speak. Keep Venutius here. I believe we will have need of him but the time is not now.'

Belatucadros hung his head and sighed. Dolnoach had never seen him so defeated. He was a strong god, a warrior god, but he had been unable to save the people most precious to him and it did not sit well. 'Do not underestimate the Roman gods' powers, for they have grown strong on the deeds of their worshippers. The more the legionnaires conquer, the stronger their gods become.'

Dolnoach felt a lump in his throat. He swallowed painfully. 'Will Boudicca succeed?'

'She has raised an army bigger than anything which has gone before. Andraste is guiding her. Boudicca's rage is strong; already she has razed towns to the ground. She was wronged by the Romans, beaten and shamed in front of her people, her daughters defiled. The Romans take no account of her husband Prasutagus's will. They would have the Iceni's lands for their own; for all that Prasutagus was their ally.'

'Cartimandua should take notice,' Dolnoach almost laughed… almost.

✳✳✳

Victory was not to be had. Boudicca's army was routed. Those not taken with the Roman way of life felt their last hope slipping away.

Venutius lived like a man in shackles. He could not do what he most wanted to. Dolnoach had been firm; the time for retaliation may come but it was not here yet. Had Cartimandua recognised her worth in the eyes of the Romans, things may have been different but, as ever, she could only see what she was gaining. Suetonius, cautious now of the strength of power the women of this island could hold, had taken to propitiating Cartimandua with expensive gifts. His ploy worked.

Cartimandua was now one of the only people native to Albion who had any time for Suetonius. He was hated so much, it was apparent even to those back in Rome that his continued presence in Britannia would only lead to further uprisings. Shortly after his defeat of Boudicca, and before he could return to the matter of silencing the Silures, he was recalled.

Britannia was now under the charge of Publius Petronius Turpilianus. Where Suetonius had been aggravating, Petronius was appeasing. Under his governorship, Britannia finally enjoyed two years of peace.

Venutius was not calmed. Cartimandua was still in control of the largest nation in Albion and giving the Romans more and more access. The few druids who had remained in Brigantia no longer felt safe. They took to their most secret nemetons and were rarely ever seen. In the ether, Brigantia wept.

Belatucadros was more hopeful. 'Keep Venutius strong,' he told Dolnoach, 'keep his connection firm with his people, but let them show no signs of dissent. The Romans are busy expanding their empire in other places; it will not be long before their fighters are needed elsewhere. If they believe Albion to be peaceable, they may well withdraw some of their legions. That will be the time to attack.'

Dolnoach nodded his agreement. Too many times people had rushed in, attacking the Romans when they were at their strongest. As frustrating as it was to withhold their enmity, the waiting game would give them victory in the end, of that he was certain.

After two years of peace, Petronius was replaced by Marcus Trebellius Maximus. Trebellius was not a military man; he improved the province's buildings, its roads and infrastructure; re-built Camulodunum, one of the key towns destroyed by Boudicca in her uprising, and increased trade in Londinium. As the province grew richer and more Romanised, it remained calm. There was no longer the need to keep four legions in Britannia and so the XIV Gemina were withdrawn, along with eight Batavian auxiliary cohorts. The remaining legionnaires were unhappy at the lack of action Britannia now offered them. They were soldiers, paid to fight. Their mood deteriorated badly.

Albion's gods watched and waited.

The air around the stones held a chill this morning. Dolnoach sat on the dry grass in the centre of the circle and waited. There would be rain later, he noted, seeing the lack of dew on the ground. He liked summer rain - it refreshed the soul. He could only think that it must be a good omen.

Belatucadros did not take long to appear and when he did, the frown that he had worn for the last ten years was gone.

'It is time.'

Dolnoach felt his stomach lurch. Excitement gripped him. 'Venutius is ready, more than ready. It has been all I could do to hold him back since the XIV legion left.'

Belatucadros stood over the druid. He did not sit, or lower himself to Dolnoach's level. That was not his way. He was too impatient, too full of energy to remain in one place for long. He rubbed a hand along one of his short, curved horns. 'Holding back is never easy but the wait has proved its worth. The Romans have descended into civil war, fighting amongst themselves. Trebellius may want peace but the soldiers want action. It is degrading for them to be acting as law enforcers and guards. What is more, Trebellius has forbidden them their schemes to impoverish our native people. It has riled the officers so much that the governor now stands accused of stealing from the army.'

Dolnoach shook his head. 'Greed is often the downfall of the ruling classes. It has tainted Cartimandua and others who have chosen to accept the yoke of Rome over the freedom of their nations. Now it even corrupts those who sought to force their will upon us.'

'Tell Venutius he must strike now, whilst the Romans are distracted amongst themselves. Trebellius has been forced to flee overseas; there will be no better time. Start with Cartimandua, oust her from the throne. Once Brigantia is taken, the north will unite and together you can march south.'

'March south?' Dolnoach was taken by surprise, unsure of what the god was saying.

Belatucadros seemed to grow larger as his temper frayed. His voice boomed over Dolnoach. 'I did not hold you back so that you could save only one nation. Venutius is not simply destined to save Brigantia, he is destined to save the whole of Albion.'

✳✳✳

Venutius dipped his rag in the ice-cold waters, closed his eyes and thought of Annagh. *Blessed Brigantia, take away her pain, ease her passing to the otherworld.* His silent prayer said, he withdrew his hand and tied the strip of cloth around one of the branches of the hawthorn tree that grew over the spring. It fluttered in the breeze along with all the other rags - in various stages of decay - which had been tied there over the years. Venutius crouched back at the water's edge and scooped up a handful of water to drink.

He could do no more. He knew beyond doubt that his mother was dying but if he could rid her of the intolerable pain she suffered night and day, it would be something. It had been a wrench leaving her; knowing that he would never see her face or speak to her again. Galchobhar had remained behind to see her safely across the void. He had grown frail himself during the years they had been in exile from Brigantia. He was old now; his body no longer fit enough to cope with the rigours of war. Venutius would miss his friend but he took solace in the fact that his mother would not die alone.

With a heavy heart, Venutius cast one last look at the clouty tree, mounted his horse and rode away. He would not return to the Carvetii lands for many years and when he did, the rag he had tied for Annagh would be long gone.

Hidden behind the trunk of the hawthorn, the deerhound watched him leave. Nodens rarely, if ever, took human form. He knew of Annagh's suffering; she was indeed dying, her body failing in ways unthinkable to the human mind. Venutius was holding all their hopes; the gods would do anything they could for him now.

Nodens waited until Venutius was out of sight before trotting off in the direction of Dunmallard. He need only to breathe on Annagh for her pain to be taken away. Galchobhar would give the hound admittance; he would recognise him for the healing god he was.

Venutius left the area with a small army at his back. The minute he crossed into Brigantian lands, the word began to spread. At last, Venuitius had risen.

His army swelled. Brigantians joined him in their thousands. Resentment at Cartimandua's treatment of both Caradoc and Venutius had not been forgotten; it had festered, along with their hatred for Vellocatus. Even the few druids who had remained in Brigantia crept out of the nemetons and marched with them.

At the high stone circle of How Tallon, they came together in a great celebration. Druids lined the circle, holding burning torches in their hands to light the darkness. In the centre, Dolnoach raised his arms skywards.

'Deae Nymphae Brigantiae,' he called. 'Hear us now.' With an outstretched arm, he pointed a finger towards the watching warriors, gathered in a ring around the stones. Turning full circle, he missed out no one. 'See these warriors, these workers and these peaceful people. They are here to free you from the shackles of the Roman scourge. The queen has forsaken her right to stand in your stead; she has no place speaking for her goddess now that she has turned her back on you. She will be routed.'

The people cheered.

At a signal from Dolnoach, two druids brought forward a prisoner. He was a Roman auxiliary; the only one of his cohort left alive. Now he was pushed onto his knees in front of Dolnoach whilst a third druid came to stand behind him. The auxiliary, wild-eyed and terrified, strained his neck to try and see what the man behind him was doing. He spoke only his native language, which poured out in a stream. Whether he was begging for mercy or praying to his own gods was unclear. The druids cared not. The man had been part of the attack on Ynys Môn and that was all that mattered.

'This land has been tainted, defiled by the presence of those who would do us harm. They have murdered our people and slaughtered many faithful druids. They have brought their own gods to our wells and holy sites, seeking to eliminate those we have held dear throughout time itself. In the names of all Albion's gods, we will drive them out!' For a man not given to shows of emotion, Dolnoach was unusually fervid. His hands trembled and tears stung his eyes. He looked down at the auxiliary as if seeing him as a man for the first time. He stared into his frightened eyes and smiled.

'I see fear, so I see weakness. Your gods cannot help you now. They will stand back and let you go. This is not your land; this is not your gods' land. This land is ours and we take it back.'

With that, the druid standing behind the auxiliary grabbed hold of the man's hair and dragged his head back. Dolnoach pulled a bone-handled dagger from within the sleeve of his robe and drew it swiftly across the man's exposed throat. He held the dagger high in the air so that everyone could see the blood-stained blade. 'The blood of the enemy is ours.'

He signalled Venutius to come forward, which he did, walking slowly into the circle. At a nod from Dolnoach, he raised his sword, and in one stroke severed the head of the auxiliary from his body. Dolnoach reached down with his empty hand and lifted the head by its hair. He held it aloft. 'The spirit of the enemy is ours.'

He held up both the knife and the head. 'The fate of the enemy is ours.' He turned in a circle, so that everyone could see. The watchers roared their approval. Someone sounded a carnyx, feet stamped and swords banged against shields. The druids raised their torches high. Dolnoach let the noise build; the louder it became, the better the omen. When it began to die away, he lowered his hands and called out once more. 'Death is not the end of living; it is merely a passageway to the afterlife. When these men set foot on Albion soil, they turned their faces towards it. In the name of all our gods, let us send them on their way.' He paused as yet more cheers sounded.

Three more druids stepped forward. The first carried a bowl of water. He poured it over the head. 'Water from Verbia's well, wash away the stain of the old and make way for the new.'

The second carried burning incense. He wafted it and for a moment the head was wreathed in smoke. 'Sage from Brigantia's land, cleanse and make ready.'

The third druid placed a clear quartz crystal into the gaping mouth. 'Crystal from Cailleach's mountain, take this life and set us free.'

Dolnoach dropped the head and lifted his voice once more. 'As the gods take this enemy, so may they take all our enemies and free our land from that which corrupts it.'

Venutius had remained in the circle, his bloodied sword still in his grasp. Now Dolnoach placed a hand on his shoulder. 'Venutius is the king chosen by the gods. He will be Brigantia's saviour. He will lead us to victory and drive out these invaders.'

The crowd went wild. Carnyces sounded and feet stamped. In the ether, the goddess Brigantia finally felt hope.

***

Vulnerability was not something Cartimandua was familiar with but now it became her constant companion. Never before had the Romans failed to aid her. She had put her trust and faith in them and they had let her down.

Not for the first time, she wished that Ostorius were still here. Then she remembered how he had been unable to cope with the constant barrage of attacks from the Silures. Let down again, she kicked out at a table leg. It hurt her foot and did nothing to calm her temper.

At the first sign of trouble, she had left Wendell and returned to Almondbury. It was a much larger fort and virtually impregnable once the great wooden gates were pulled closed. She paced up and down, her concerns growing every time she was brought news of yet another defeat. Her servants cowered, not wanting to approach her and feel the bite of her temper.

Cartimandua called on her priests for advice. They had no Augur and since they were the only priests permitted to read the signs of the gods, she felt blinded. She began to wonder if she had been right to let the druids withdraw. Not all were as admonishing as Galchobhar. She shivered as she thought of her old druid, remembering the curse he had hurled at her years before. That curse had been given here at Almondbury; maybe it had sat waiting for her to return? The downy hairs on her body stood on end. She shivered again and called for wine. A young servant came running and set the jug and glass before her with trembling hands. Cartimandua sent her from the room and poured the drink herself. She had no time to mollycoddle the timid and she certainly did not want to end up with wine down her expensive dress.

She took a sip and swore loudly. Outside the

room, the servant cringed. Not waiting for the summons, she hurried away to fetch an alternative. This time, she poured the wine from a freshly unsealed amphora. She hurried back to her mistress and was saved from her savage tongue by a commotion outside. Vellocatus had arrived, bringing with him a number of soldiers - all that was left of his army. He left the soldiers waiting just inside the gate and ran calling for his wife. His face was tight and covered in mud; a large cut patterned his upper arm and his armour bore signs of heavy use.

The servant almost dropped the wine in her haste. She placed it on the table, grabbed the unwanted jug and rushed from the room. The atmosphere was not one in which to linger and she wanted to be as far away as possible when Vellocatus delivered what was obviously going to be bad news.

Cartimandua stared at him in disbelief. 'What has happened, why are you not out with your army?' Stupidly, hope flowered; she risked a smile, 'Is Venutius dead?'

Vellocatus slammed his fist down onto the table, sending the wine jug crashing to the floor. 'We are beaten. Venutius has the upper hand and the strength. Our soldiers fled to him in their droves. They would not follow me; even some of the auxiliaries refused to take my command. We are defeated, my love, all we can do is flee. I have come to take you to safety.'

The queen could not find her voice. Her

mouth opened and closed but no sound came out.
She reached for her glass but she had already
thrown the sour wine away and it stood empty.
Her legs wobbled and threatened to buckle.
Vellocatus crossed the space between them in one
stride and gathered her in his arms.

'Far better to leave now and prepare to return
later than to stay and be swallowed up by the tidal
wave that is following.' He ran a curled finger up
her throat and under her chin, dropping his head
to place a kiss on her lips. He was sweaty and hot
but Cartimandua could not have cared less. He
had come to rescue her. She had been right to put
her faith in the Romans, after all.

When Venutius reached Almondbury, he wasted
no time vying for an audience with Cartimandua.
He had heard and seen enough in the past to
know that there could be no reasoning with her.
His army hit the fort without mercy; anyone not
turning to fight alongside the attackers was cut
down and left where they fell. The fort gates were
swung wide and though the auxiliaries and what
remained of Vellocatus's army put up a desperate
fight, they could not withstand the onslaught.
Both the fort and the surrounding houses were
soon reduced to burning ruins. In the ferocity of
the attack, no one could say what had happened
to the queen. Some thought they had seen her,
fighting for her life in the great hall; others
claimed it was only a serving girl who happened to
have the same dark brown hair.

Venutius watched the fort burning. If Cartimandua and her low-born husband were still inside, there would be no chance of their survival. His victory had not exactly been easy but it had been a great deal more straightforward than expected. Bolstered, he began to think seriously about what Dolnoach had said to him. Could he do it? Could he take on the whole of the Roman army?

He looked at the warriors supporting him; men and women who had fought so hard to be free of the tyranny that their traitorous queen and the oppressive Romans had brought. Their faces said more than any words could convey. He closed his eyes, knowing that if he stopped now, freedom would soon be taken away from them. The Romans would sort themselves out and they would send another governor. They would never stand for another rebellion in the north. Taking a deep breath, he silently called out, *Brigantia, High One and guardian of our lands. Send me a sign that I should go on fighting.*

He heard nothing in response. Disappointed, but not in the least bit surprised, he opened his eyes. From the corner of his vision, he noticed something moving, bobbing up and down on the thin branches of a willow tree. The little bird fluttered onto his arm and hopped down to his hand. Its eyes were no bigger than the smallest glass bead, its cocked tail sticking upright as if it were not big enough to balance without it. He had never seen a wren so close. He knew that they were small birds but he could barely feel any weight on his palm at all.

As Venutius watched, it opened its thin little beak and began to sing the song of the woodland. It was a sound that always made him feel at peace. It filled his body and flowed through his veins as liquid calm. That such a tiny bird could produce so big a sound was amazing. The wren flew up to his shoulder and sang again. Venutius could not help but smile. He had asked for a sign - and what could be clearer? Galchobhar had always told him Brigantia watched her people in the guise of a wren. The old druid would have been astounded at this display.

'Do you want me to keep going?' he whispered to the bird. She tilted her head to the side, as if listening, then sang again. Venutius held out his finger and the wren hopped onto it. He lifted it nearer to his face. The beady eyes, he realised, had a strange hint of colour to them. They were not quite the eyes of an ordinary bird. There was depth to them; so much depth that he could have fallen right in and been lost.

The thought startled him; you could not possibly fall into something so minuscule - you could be enveloped by the love of a goddess, though, he reasoned. The wren cocked her head again and flicked her tail. Venutius understood. He smiled at the bird. *We are going to fight.*

✳✳✳

Further south, the Romans were in disarray. When Venutius swept down on them, they were unprepared, too busy fighting amongst themselves to order a cohesive defence. They had expected a small army of Brigantians. What Venutius brought with him was a conglomeration of northern nations.

Whilst Almondbury was still burning, he had sent messengers to the adjoining nations, garnering support. They had not disappointed. The druids, it seemed, had urged the importance of ridding the land of the vermin Romans. All the northern nations bar the Votadini fell behind Venutius in their droves. Finally, what was left of Albion had risen up, almost as one.

Many of the southern nations that had initially been swallowed up into the Britannia province stood back and refused to fight - on any side. They were too frightened of the Romans' wrath. Their nations had been torn apart in retaliation for their former opposition and many of the lower classes were still suffering. Once they saw how strong the army of the north was, and how weak the legionnaires were in response, they threw off their reservations and took up arms. It was the final straw for the Romans. With no help coming from overseas, they turned tail and fled.

✳✳✳

Venutius was hailed the saviour of Albion. The rulers of the other nations vied for the chance to carry him aloft on their shoulders. He suffered their praise for a day or two and then he took his warriors and headed for home.

Back in Brigantia, he made Stanwick his base. It was the fort closest to the Votadini lands. He was wary of that nation. On the surface they were amenable enough but they had been close allies of the Romans. They had chosen not to fight alongside their Albion neighbours and Venutius doubted that they would give up their close ties to the empire. He left Almondbury in its ruinous state. It held the ghosts of his former life. He had no desire to see it rebuilt.

Galchobhar made the journey from Dunmallard. Venutius was shocked to see how much his friend had deteriorated.

'Do not waste your concerns on me,' the druid told him, 'I have had a good life. It has been an honour to spend a large part of it at your side. You have done more for Albion than you can ever realise, my friend.'

Venutius frowned. 'You sound as if you are dying? Was my mother's death not enough?'

'Annagh's death was a blessing. She struggled to hang on until she had heard how you fared against Cartimandua. I have never known anyone so determined. Her pain may have left her but her body had long since given up.'

Venutius had to smile. 'She always was stubborn.' His smile faded. He would miss her; his mother was a good woman, she had not deserved such a pitiful passing.

'I will not be here much longer,' Galchobhar admitted, 'I hear Cailleach beginning to call me.' He held his hand up when Venutius made to interrupt. 'I have time to put my affairs in order and to see you crowned once more. The old yew tree, Ioho, will stand watch over proceedings. He has seen many lives come and go and will see many more before his time is done. The gods feel safe within his bows; they will be lining up to watch as I place the torc around your neck.'

Venutius rubbed a hand across his nape. He had missed feeling the weight of his torc. The heavy gold served as a constant reminder of the burdens he carried as king. 'I hope I can do the gods justice this time.'

'They have faith in you, my friend. They chose you for a reason.'

Venutius sighed. 'I will make sure the errors that were made in this land are remembered as a warning. Never again must the Romans get the chance to return. The people will not be allowed to forget. Cartimandua will go down in history, as the traitor who almost lost us everything.'

Galchobhar nodded his agreement. 'Thank the gods she is dead.'

'Aye,' Venutius agreed. 'She can do no more harm now.'

***

On the rough seas, the Roman trading ship battled against the angry waves. The storm had come upon them almost as soon as they had left the Votadini shore. Vellocatus paid no mind to the rolling deck. He loved the movement of the boat beneath his feet. It was the first time in weeks that he had felt something akin to happiness. They had been lucky to escape from Almondbury. Disguised, the pair of them had slipped out of the gates barely a moment before Venutius's army had appeared. They had not looked back. It was a long way to the safety of the Votadini lands.

Cartimandua had not eaten since they had left port yet still her stomach roiled. Beside her, the Augur watched the skies. Sea birds swirled overhead. They had met him at Dumpender Law, capital of the Votadini. He too was heading back to Rome, taking word of the continued friendship of the Votadini king. In his hand he held bolas - two stones tied together with a strip of leather. Suddenly, he threw them skyward. They wrapped around the neck of a sad-looking bird with a brightly striped bill. The bird crashed down onto the boat.

Whilst it was still breathing, the Augur scooped it up and slit open its belly. The entrails slid out onto the deck. He studied them carefully, a cruel smile appearing on his thoughtful face. Just then, the boat lurched on a high wave and the entrails were thrown across the boards. The Augur cursed, his reading lost.

'What did it say?' Cartimandua demanded.

'It said you will not return to Albion.'

Cartimandua clung hold of the side of the boat, her face white with seasickness and fury. The Augur pointed his finger at her. 'You will not return to Albion,' he repeated, 'but one day, your descendant shall.'

The End

Find out what happens when Cartimandua's descendant finally arrives in Brigantia to challenge for the throne.

The Girl of Two Worlds

NEVER UNDERESTIMATE THE POWER OF THE GODS.

Kariss is struggling, her past is vague and her future uncertain. London is not a place to live, alone and afraid. When a strange old woman suddenly offers her a change, Kariss eagerly accepts.

The ancient goddess Cailleach knows Kariss. It was she who brought her to this world and hid her memories. Here, long ago, the Romans were victorious, Britannia endured and Albion's gods had been driven to obscurity. There could be no safer place to hide someone so important.

Now though Kariss must return to Albion. She might not remember yet but she is the joint heir to the Brigante throne. Her rival, Martaani has already arrived; she has the Romans behind her and will stop at nothing to win back all that her ancestor, Cartimandua lost.

Many years ago, the gods were complacent. They did not understand the dangers of the Romans. They will not make the same mistake again.

As Kariss learns the secret of her life and the destiny prophesied at her birth, will she find the strength to endure all that the gods must put her through?

The Albion Chronicles:

Queen of Betrayal

The Girl of Two Worlds

Seven Druids

The Battle for Brigantia

For news on these and other titles by Nelly Harper visit:

www.nellyharper.co.uk
www.goblinhouse.co.uk

Did you enjoy this story?
If so, please consider leaving a review on Amazon and/or Goodreads.
Reviews are vital to authors. They tell them what they are doing right, and what can be improved upon. They also help potential readers chose books they will enjoy.

Reviews do not need to be in-depth. Just say what you liked about the story and why you liked it.
Please remember to avoid spoilers.

Also by Nelly Harper:

The Jet Necklace

A POWERFUL SPELL, ONCE UNLEASHED WILL
NOT STOP UNTIL ITS WORK IS DONE.

~ However long it takes ~

Centuries have passed since the jet necklace was made
and imbued with a magical calming spell capable of
stopping even the strongest hate and hostility.

Oonagh is forced to flee the invading Vikings, hiding the
necklace from them as she runs. With everyone she
knows dead, she builds a new life far away from the
troubles.

When an act of ultimate betrayal brings the past crashing
back, her daughter Bethoc, must return to her mother's
homeland and try to retrieve the necklace before it is too
late.

www.ingramcontent.com/pod-product-compliance
Lightning Source LLC
Chambersburg PA
CBHW021742190726
48288CB00009B/3135